SOMETHING'S
IN THE WOODS

CHOOSE YOUR OWN NIGHTMARE

titles in Large-Print Editions:

#1 NIGHT OF THE WEREWOLF

#2 BEWARE THE SNAKE'S VENOM

#3 ISLAND OF DOOM

#4 CASTLE OF DARKNESS

#5 THE HALLOWEEN PARTY

#6 RISK YOUR LIFE ARCADE

#7 BITING FOR BLOOD

#8 BUGGED OUT!

#9 THE MUMMY WHO WOULDN'T DIE

#10 IT HAPPENED AT CAMP PINE TREE

#11 WATCH OUT FOR ROOM 13

#12 SOMETHING'S IN THE WOODS

CHOOSE YOUR OWN NIGHTMARE #12

SOMETHING'S IN THE WOODS

by Richard Brightfield

ILLUSTRATED BY BILL SCHMIDT

An Edward Packard Book

Gareth Stevens Publishing
MILWAUKEE

For a free color catalog describing Gareth Stevens' list of high-quality books
and multimedia programs, call 1-800-542-2595 (USA) or 1-800-461-9120
(Canada). Gareth Stevens Publishing's Fax: (414) 225-0377.
See our catalog, too, on the World Wide Web: http://gsinc.com

Library of Congress Cataloging-in-Publication Data

Brightfield, Rick.
    Something's in the woods / by Richard Brightfield ; illustrated by
 Bill Schmidt.
       p. cm. — (Choose your own nightmare; #12)
    Summary: The reader's decisions control the course of an adventure
 in the woods involving spooky ghost kids, disappearing parents,
 underground goblins, and mind-blowing time warps.
    ISBN 0-8368-1724-9 (lib. bdg.)
    1. Plot-your-own stories. [1. Horror stories. 2. Plot-your-own
 stories.] I. Schmidt, Bill, ill. II. Title. III. Series.
 PZ7.B76523So   1997
 [Fic]—dc20   96-31016

This edition first published in 1997 by
Gareth Stevens Publishing
1555 North RiverCenter Drive, Suite 201
Milwaukee, Wisconsin 53212 USA

Printed in the United States of America

1 2 3 4 5 6 7 8 9 01 00 99 98 97

SOMETHING'S IN THE WOODS

WARNING!

You have probably read books where scary things happen to people. Well, in *Choose Your Own Nightmare*, you're right in the middle of the action. The scary things are happening to you!

Wiley Woods is totally weird. Creepy goblins that live underground, spooky ghost kids, disappearing parents, and mind-blowing time warps! You're in for a night your friends won't *believe*!

Don't forget—YOU control your fate. Only you can decide what happens. Follow the instructions at the bottom of each page. The thrills and chills that happen to you will depend on your choices!

Something strange is definitely going on in this woods. And it's time you find out what it is. So turn to page 1 and *CHOOSE YOUR OWN NIGHTMARE*!

2345678901234567890

1

"Hey! Wasn't that the entrance to the park?" you ask as you speed by a sign overgrown with bushes.

You and your parents are in your minivan heading for Wiley Woods. It's a state park about a two-hour drive from your house. Your dad camped here when he was a kid. You're sitting in the backseat, watching the scenery flash by.

"I think you're right," your dad says. He makes a broad U-turn and heads back. Sure enough, the sign says WILEY WOODS. It is propped against a large, dumbbell-shaped rock. Your dad turns down the dirt road next to it.

"The park *is* open, isn't it?" asks your mom as the minivan bounces down the road. It's filled with deep ruts and sprinkled with weeds.

"I'm not sure," your dad says. "But that looks like a gatehouse up ahead. We'll find out."

Turn to page 2.

2

Your dad stops the minivan under a dilapidated archway built out from a small gatehouse. You can see that the gatehouse was once painted white, but most of the paint has peeled off, exposing dark, weather-beaten wood underneath.

A very thin, bearded man in a tattered blue shirt leans out of a window facing into the archway. His skin is wrinkled and toughened, and he's missing quite a few teeth. He looks surprised to see you.

"What do you want?" he asks suspiciously.

"Is the park open?" your dad inquires.

"Ah . . . I guess so," says the man after a slight hesitation. His eyes dart from you to your dad to your mom. Then back to you.

"We'd like to go camping," your dad says firmly.

"That's all right with me. I mean if you really want to," the gatekeeper says, stroking his scraggly beard. "I can see that you people ain't from around here."

Go to page 4.

"Is something wrong with the park?" your mom asks worriedly.

The gatekeeper lets out a strange, high-pitched laugh. It makes you nervous. "Well, people in these parts think it's haunted. Won't come near it with a ten-foot pole," he says slowly. "There have been some pretty wild stories about people disappearing, ghosts floating around." He shrugs. "Pretty much nonsense, if you ask me."

Is it your imagination, or did he just wink at you? Maybe he's right—maybe Wiley Woods *is* haunted!

"Do you think we should turn around and—" your mom starts to say.

"Haunted?" your dad interrupts. "That old legend?" He peers around the gatehouse. "Which way is the lake? I want to do some fishing."

"Hmmm." The gatekeeper thinks. "Just keep going down this road about half a mile, then bear left where the road forks and . . . no, maybe you go right." He looks confused.

Go on to the next page.

"You'd better ask the park ranger. He's in there," the gatekeeper finally says, pointing to a small two-story building a short distance away.

"Okay, thanks," your dad says, starting up the minivan again and heading down the road. The ranger's building is in the same state of disrepair as the gatehouse. Its high-pitched roof sags in the middle. The door's paint is chipped and peeling. A small plaque above the doorknob says INFORMATION.

You and your mom get out and stretch your legs while your dad knocks on the door.

Out of the corner of your eye you glimpse a figure moving in the upstairs window. It looks like a girl.

"I see someone upstairs!" you exclaim.

Your dad knocks several more times. "Well, no one's answering."

"Your eyes must be playing tricks on you," your mom tells you. "The place is empty."

"We'll find the lake on our own," says your dad.

You're mad. You know you saw something.

Cross your arms and turn to page 15.

6

Your head begins to spin, and you're afraid you might faint. You *did* enter some kind of time warp! These people are not in costumes. They're for real.

You swallow. "Well, if it's not a joke, don't I get a trial or something?" you ask in a tiny voice.

"A trial? Now ain't you the fancy one. Comin' in here all high and mighty, eatin' me food, then tryin' to pawn off counterfeit money on me."

"But—but that's a real dime—ten cents," you protest weakly.

"Don't make it worse for yourself by lyin'!" the tavern keeper yells angrily. Other customers begin to look your way with interest. "A false coin is the work of the devil, and lyin' is the speech of the devil. You wait right here while I get the sheriff," he says before striding out the door.

You tap your fingers nervously on the table. How are you going to get out of this mess?

Don't move an inch—except to page 10.

Run for it to page 28.

You stand there for a few minutes, wondering what to do.

Crankety-crank-a-crank. A rumbling sound comes from around a bend in the road. You jump back into the bushes as a train of painted wagons appears around the bend.

You watch as they roll by. Then you recognize Carlo's wagon.

"Hey!" you cry, running out and jumping on the back platform. You look through the window and see lantern light inside.

Rap, rap, rap. "Carlo! It's me. Let me in!" you whisper.

The door opens a crack. It's Carlo. He looks surprised to see you. Then he gives you a broad smile.

"I want to take you up on your offer to join you, at least until we get someplace where I can call my grandparents," you say.

"Great," Carlo says, motioning for you to come in.

"That village back there was awful," you tell him. "You wouldn't believe what happened to me."

Turn to page 21.

8

Your heart starts to beat fast. You are thinking of what Carlo told you about the forest. That it does funny things with time.

Could you be in some sort of weird time warp?

Holding your chest, you lean against the ladder.

This can't be happening! you think in a panic. Stuff like this only happens on TV. Or in books you've read in school.

School . . . All at once it hits you. This must be one of those restored villages that some of the state parks have. A teacher in school once told your class about them. And your mom was talking about a village just like this yesterday. You breathe a sigh of relief. You're at one of those places. Maybe your parents will be here!

Hurry to page 33.

Sometime during the night, a strange noise wakes you. It sounds as if an animal is in front of your tent!

You are about to cry out when you realize that the sound is only the wind blowing the tent flaps and rustling through the trees outside.

You try to go back to sleep, but the wind sounds like voices—voices of children lost in the forest. Like the ones in your dad's story, you think unhappily.

The story sounded dumb before—but it's got you nervous now.

Suddenly you get an overwhelming urge to join your parents—whether they like it or not. You crawl out of your tent and into the silvery moonlight.

But something's wrong. It takes you a few seconds to realize that your parents' tent is no longer there.

It's vanished!

You run around the clearing in a panic. "Mom! Dad! Where are you?" you cry out.

Hurry to page 35.

10

You decide to wait for the sheriff—maybe you can talk your way out of this like you do when your teacher at school tries to punish you. A few minutes later the tavern keeper returns, accompanied by a tall, heavyset man dressed in a plaid shirt and twill pants. His long black hair is tied back in a ponytail. He has the longest mustache you've ever seen. You don't see any sign of a badge, but he must be the sheriff.

"So this is the culprit," the sheriff drawls, chewing on the ends of his mustache. He grabs you by the ear and drags you out of the tavern.

"Ouch!" you cry. It really hurts. "Hey! You don't have to tear my ear off!"

"All right," he says, letting go. "But don't get any funny ideas about getting away."

The sheriff pushes you down the cobblestoned street to a small stone building with iron bars on the windows. He unlocks the heavy oak door with a large key.

Go to page 53.

You move cautiously along the narrow trail. "Mom?" you whisper. "Dad?"

No reply.

You stop and listen. You can't hear the voices anymore, but you do hear rustling in the nearby bushes. A low, growling sound. Not human.

A thin shaft of pale moonlight illuminates a small clearing just ahead.

Slowly, you push through the remaining bushes. Something is crouched on the other side of the clearing. Waiting. A black shape with two glowing yellow eyes stares out at you.

Oh no! Turn to page 61.

12

You crawl over and pull yourself up to the windowsill. It doesn't look too far to the ground. But looks can be deceiving.

A thick vine is growing just outside the window. You pull your feet up, slip out the window, and go down, hand over hand. When you are almost to the ground, your bare feet touch something soft and furry.

"Oh!" you blurt out. You climb a short way back up the vine, swing to one side, and jump clear.

When you are safely on the ground, you stare at the furry shape. It's that weird girl's pet—Algenon. It's sleeping with one large paw over its face. It shifts in its sleep, breathing heavily.

Hurriedly you tiptoe across the field. Just as you reach the edge of the woods, Algenon wakes up and growls. It jumps up and starts after you.

You dash into the woods as the animal bounds across the field. You wish you had your shoes, but somehow not having them on helps you to run faster. You can hear Algenon crashing through the bushes behind you.

Quick! Hurry to page 37.

Suddenly you emerge from the woods and find yourself at the edge of an overgrown field that stretches away in the moonlight. You spy a building in the distance. It's the park information center.

You move toward the building. Inside, upstairs, you can see a man and a woman arguing. They shake their fists at each other. The woman is much bigger than the man.

You swallow. It isn't your parents. Your dad is taller than your mom.

You move closer. For some reason you are tiptoeing—even though there's no one around to see you.

"Hello," whispers a soft voice behind you. You nearly jump out of your skin as someone pulls at your sleeve.

"Wha—!" you scream, clutching your chest.

A small girl with pale skin and sickly yellowish eyes stands behind you. You wonder if she's the girl you saw earlier in the window of the information center. You *knew* you weren't imagining things.

Discover who she is on page 49.

14

You scramble to your feet and try desperately to climb back up. But it's no use. It's too slippery.

And you can't see a thing. It's pitch-dark.

"Hee hee hee! Another one!" cackles a voice in the darkness. It's the strangest-sounding voice you've ever heard. You look behind you and see a very short man, wearing a close-fitting cap and red velveteen breeches, standing a few feet away. His ears are pointed, and instead of front teeth he has a little pair of fangs.

"Who *are* you?" you ask.

He chortles. "Never mind that. The important thing is that you fell for my trap. You just couldn't resist the crystal ball, could you?"

You feel an icy chill of terror. This is no ordinary man. He's a goblin! You've been tricked! And caught!

Turn to page 62.

You all get back in the minivan and continue down the rocky road. Fifteen minutes later, it divides into two small paths. A rustic signpost on the right path reads TO THE LAKE.

"See?" says your dad triumphantly. "I had a hunch it was this way." He pulls over and parks the minivan. Then he unloads the backpacks. You sling the straps of yours over your shoulders.

"I brought along a small tent for you," your mom tells you as you start down the thread-like path to the lake.

"You mean I'm going to have to sleep in a tent all by myself?" You moan.

"We thought you'd *like* that," your mom says. "We'll put it real close to ours."

"Well . . . okay," you grumble.

You hike along for another fifteen minutes. Then the path turns even narrower. Off to one side, down a steep slope, is a bubbling stream. Within minutes you come out into a wide clearing. A small waterfall tumbles from a cliff into the lake.

Run ahead and turn to page 46.

16

"No way!" you say. You push past him and tear out of the building. You run at high speed for several minutes until you reach a paved road. Headlights shine in the distance. You wave frantically as they approach. But instead of stopping, the vehicle speeds up and races by you.

Using your excellent sense of direction, you find your way back to your campsite. But all the while you have a feeling that you are being followed.

When you get back to the campsite, you're amazed to find both your tent and your parents', side by side.

You unzip your parents' tent. There they are. Snoring, side by side. What a relief. You crawl into your tent and quickly fall asleep.

When you wake up in the morning, a large, furry animal is curled up next to you. It's Algenon! You crawl out of the tent.

"Mom! Dad!" you cry. "Come quick!"

Go to page 48.

"I don't think so," you say.

"Don't be too hasty," says the girl. "Once you're lost in Wiley Woods, you never find your way out." She floats over to you and touches your hand. Her hand goes right through yours. Her touch feels like ice water.

Turn to page 82.

18

Suddenly Amanda gives you a big shove from behind. You stumble inside. The man moves like a flash, slamming the door shut behind you and pressing himself against it.

"Hey!" you exclaim. "What do you think you're doing?" You look at Amanda. Who would have thought she was so strong?

An old-fashioned wooden desk sits in the corner. Piles of papers are stacked on top of it. There are a few chairs scattered about the room and a lopsided coffee table covered with magazines. A big, yellowed map of the park is taped to the wall.

"You shouldn't be outside," the woman says. You try not to stare as she picks at her teeth. "The goblins come out on moonlit nights."

"Yeah, that's right," says the man. He points to the map. "Want to see where they like to hang out?"

You shake your head. Goblins, goblins, goblins! You're really sick of hearing about them. This family is really strange. You've got to get out of here.

Take a deep breath and turn to page 52.

20

You drop the map on the ground, but the shocked feeling stays with you. You try to head for the front door. But you find yourself walking toward the stairs. You march up them like a robot. What's happening? Your mind is in a panic! You can't seem to control your body! The others follow you up.

You take off your shoes at the top of the stairs. Then you turn left into a small room. A four-poster bed covered with a quilt sits in the center of the room. Streams of moonlight shine through a tall window onto the foot of the bed.

"Lie down!" the woman orders.

You don't want to, but your body obeys her command. The quilt wraps around and grabs hold of you.

"Sleep tight," Amanda says, closing the door to the room.

The bed is comfortable in a strange sort of way—even though you don't want to be there. You *are* tired. Maybe you'll wake up rested and be able to get this mess straightened out.

Catch a few winks. Then turn to page 64.

Or put up a fight and turn to page 54.

"I know," Carlo says. "I heard you caused quite a stir. If you really want to pass phony money, you'd better let me teach you how to do it."

"I wasn't trying to pass phony money!" you exclaim. You start to tell Carlo the whole story but change your mind. It would take too long.

"I can train you to be a juggler. How would you like that?" Carlo says.

"Yeah, whatever," you say, slumping against the side of the wagon. You remember the day your parents told you that you were all going to Wiley Woods. You were so happy. What a big mistake that turned out to be.

Early the next morning, the caravan stops along the road to feed and water the horses. You get out to stretch your legs.

Bending down, you notice a rock. It's the dumbbell-shaped rock that was at the entrance to the state park! You must be near your campsite!

Quick! Turn to page 69.

22

You manage to get one leg free. You push yourself up with all your strength and slide off the bed. Now you're wedged in the narrow space between the bed and the wall.

As you start to squeeze around the side, the quilt heaves up and blocks your way.

"Sorry, but it's not my bedtime," you mutter as you dive down and roll under the bed. There's just enough space for you to fit.

This quilt is driving you crazy. You could try to crawl toward the door—or make your escape through the window, even though you're on the second floor.

If you try the window,
turn to page 12.

If you think you'd better use the door,
turn to page 60.

"Sure, I'll come over to the center if you really think your mom and dad can help me," you say. "But I don't want to go inside."

The girl takes you by the hand and pulls you toward the center. The dog—or bear, or whatever it is—follows along behind.

The front door of the center opens, throwing a long rectangle of yellow light into the night. The man and woman who were arguing have come downstairs and are silhouetted in the doorway. The man is wearing a faded brown uniform. His greasy brown hair hangs in his face. He must be the park ranger. The woman is dressed in a similar uniform. Her teeth are dirty and chipped. She's about five inches taller than the man.

"Come in, come in," the woman says. She turns to the little girl. "You made a new friend, Amanda. Goody for you!" Then she pats your arm. "Would you like to watch some TV?"

"No, I can't. Listen, I'm in trouble. My parents—"

Flip back fast to page 18.

24

You don't really feel like explaining your situation to total strangers.

You sigh. Where could your parents be? There must be a good explanation for all this.

Shoulders drooping, you go back and sit cross-legged in front of your tent, listening to the sound of the nearby waterfall. Gradually your eyes get used to the darkness. The stars shine like ornaments through the tree branches over your head.

Off to the left you see a series of flashes. They're really bright. You hear a strange clicking sound from the same direction. What could it be? Is it the park ranger?

You jump to your feet and edge a short way into the bushes. The flashes are brighter now. Should you investigate the lights or not? You don't want to get too far away from your tent. But you *have* to find your parents.

Check it out on page 42.

*If you decide to stay where you are,
turn to page 32.*

You scramble out and look around. A large, furry shape is crouching on the other side of the tent, sniffing and pawing the ground. It's a bear!

The bear backs into your tent. You stand there, too shocked to move. You've heard about bears attacking campers—but you never thought it would actually happen to you. A few seconds later, the bear comes barreling out, holding about seven of your candy bars in its mouth.

You'd better get out of here!

You race over to the nearest tree, climbing up as high as you can.

You can't believe you've had such a narrow escape. This bear could kill you in a flash. His teeth are huge.

The bear eyes you for a few seconds. Then it starts to amble back into the woods.

"Thank goodness," you say, beginning to climb down.

Suddenly the bear turns around and heads back your way. You scramble back up into the tree.

Grin and bear it on page 34.

26

You emerge from the woods and head for the campfire. Several of the dancers notice you and give you friendly smiles. A boy dressed like a court jester motions for you to come over. He looks about your age. He has a mop of black hair and large brown eyes.

"My name is Carlo," he says. "You come to join our merry band?"

"Uh, no," you say, feeling a bit unsure. "I'm trying to find my parents. We're here camping and I woke up and they were gone." You describe your mom and dad to Carlo. "You haven't seen them, have you?"

"No, sorry. We've been here since sunset."

"I've got to find them!" you say, choking back a sob.

Carlo pats your arm. "Maybe with luck they will find *you,*" he says. "Would you like something to eat? That large iron pot by the fire is full of stew. Not much meat in it, but some good potatoes."

"Stew? I—I don't know . . . ," you say, hesitating. You usually don't like other people's cooking, but you are pretty hungry.

Take a deep sniff and turn to page 31.

The man frowns. "Ignore that," he says. But the pounding continues. Finally the woman opens the door. It's your parents.

"Look, we're not interested in buying anything," says the woman. She tries to keep them from seeing you, but it's no use.

"That's our kid!" your mom yells, shoving the woman out of the way. The man and Amanda have run upstairs.

"This is disgraceful!" your mom exclaims. "In a state park, of all things."

"Right!" your dad says. "I'm going to sue you people over this!"

Your parents untie you and help you get to your feet.

"Let's get out of here!" you say, running toward the door. The woman is sitting on the couch.

"All we wanted was a tasty stew," she says apologetically.

Your mom glares at her. "Next time, try some pepper!"

The End

28

None of the tavern customers is looking your way. You jump up from the table and dash out the door.

The tavern keeper is already a good way down the street. Just beyond him is the stage Carlo and his companions have erected. Most of the townspeople are gathered there to watch the play.

The tavern keeper looks back just as you start running the other way. "Stop, thief!" he hollers. He turns and starts running back after you.

Run to page 81.

"American?" the boy repeats.

"As in 'The United States of America,' " you say, your voice rising in anger.

The boy snaps his fingers. "You're one of them revolutionaries I done heard about!" he says. "They'll hang you for that, too."

He sticks out his hand for you to shake. "Nice to meet a revolutionary. What's your name? I'm Joshua."

You tell him your name. "This is ridiculous," you say.

"That it be," Joshua says. "They're hangin' me for stealin' a loaf of bread, and hangin' Timothy over there for takin' a chicken."

"They can't do that. They haven't done that since the seventeenth century," you say.

Everyone in the cell bursts into laughter.

"This *is* the seventeenth century!" one of them says.

The seventeenth century! It's even worse than you thought!

Time-warp it to page 41.

"It's very good. We gather herbs and wild vegetables in the forest. We catch ducks, too, and sometimes get free chickens in the towns where we perform."

"I think I'll pass," you say.

"Okay," Carlo says. "But sit here by the fire."

"Look," you plead. "This is serious. My parents would never deliberately leave me stranded in the woods. I'm worried that something's happened to them. Can't you and your friends help me?"

"I don't know," he says. "We have traveled through these woods many times and seen many things. There are evil forces here. I too hope nothing bad has happened to your parents."

"Like what?" you ask. You are getting really worried now.

"The forest does things with time. Funny things." Carlo frowns. "And there are strange beings on the ground and below it."

"Like—like goblins?" you ask, feeling kind of foolish. "I'm not sure I believe in them."

Hurry to page 55.

32

You decide to stay where you are. You go back to where your parents pitched their tent. It's hard to see in the dim light, but you can make out a large circular hole.

You lean over the edge and look down. Suddenly the ground drops out from under your feet.

"Ahhh!" you scream at the top of your lungs as you plunge into the hole.

Luckily you manage to grab on to some kind of tree root. You hang there for a few minutes, gasping for breath. Then, using all your strength, you dig your feet into the side of the hole and pull yourself up and out.

You collapse on the ground, taking short, rasping breaths.

"Help! Help!"

Your ears perk up. The voices are coming from down in the hole. It's your mom and dad!

"Mom! Dad!" you cry, peering into the darkness. "Don't worry, I'll get you out!"

Turn to page 39.

Carlo opens the door in the back of the wagon and comes inside. "You are awake," he says. "We are just entering Dunston and—"

Suddenly the wagon stops. You can see through the window that a crowd is gathering around it. The people are all dressed in colonial costumes. You recognize them from pictures you've seen in school.

"What's happening out there?" you ask.

"We're going to set up our stage for the afternoon performance of *The Comedy of Errors* by the Bard of Avon," Carlo explains.

"Bard of Avon?" you repeat.

Carlo laughs. "Shakespeare, of course."

"I've heard of him," you say.

"I hope you will watch our performance," Carlo says. "Right now, I must go and take care of the horses. Perhaps you will see your parents here. If not, you can stay with us."

"That's awfully nice of you, but I really need to get back home," you tell him. "Thanks for the ride." You run your fingers through your hair, trying to make yourself presentable.

"Sure," he says. "Good luck."

Push on ahead to page 67.

You watch as the bear sits down directly below you. It stuffs your candy bars into its mouth and then looks up at you. It gives a low, mean growl.

You swallow hard.

Will your parents come back? Or will you be stuck up in this tree all night?

Looks like you'll be stuck here—unless you want to start over again at the beginning of the book. Because this is . . .

The End

The echo of your voice comes back from the direction of the waterfall. But there's no answer from your parents.

I must be dreaming, you think. I'll pinch myself. If I'm asleep, I'll wake up. At least that's what your grandma always tells you.

"Ouch!" you cry out as you pinch your leg. Nothing happens. You are still standing in the clearing. Alone.

"What's going on here?" you shout. Silence.

Your parents wouldn't have moved their tent without telling you.

Unless something terrible has happened.

Then you hear something. Voices. Coming from the trail that leads back to where the minivan is parked. Mom and Dad! You run toward the sound—you've never been so glad to hear your mom's whiny voice in your life. But then you stop short. Maybe it's not your parents. Maybe it's the park ranger. Or some other campers. Crazy ones.

You don't care who it is—you can't stand being alone! Turn to page 11.

Chill by the tent and turn to page 24.

36

A rumble goes through the camp as more of the horse-drawn wagons start to pull out. You wonder why they don't use trucks or cars. The park roads must be too bumpy for them.

"I'll go with you," you tell Carlo.

"Great! Come on!" he says, running after one of the wagons. You hurry behind him. When you get to the wagon, you both jump onto a platform on the back. You hold on as the wagon bounces along the trail through the woods. In a few minutes, you've left the campfire behind and have only the moonlight to see by.

"Let's go inside and get some rest," Carlo says, yawning.

You follow him through the door in the back of the covered wagon. To your surprise, Carlo lights a lantern. Everything about these people is so old-fashioned. It must be part of their act.

"I guess you save a lot of money and energy, using those," you say, pointing to the lantern. Carlo gives you a funny look.

"You're a strange one," he says, laughing.

Head over to page 75.

You are about to give up all hope when you stumble onto a dirt road. It looks like the road that runs from the park entrance to your camp. You run along it as fast as you can. Up ahead, you see your minivan parked off to the side. You hope your dad didn't lock it.

Your bare feet fly over the ground. You reach the minivan, dive inside, and slam the door just as Algenon crashes into it.

You crouch inside in fear as Algenon grabs the door handle with its teeth and tries to yank the door open. When that doesn't work, it jumps up on the hood and attacks the windshield with its claws, snarling in rage.

Suddenly it stops. A huge, catlike animal is crouching at the edge of the woods. Algenon growls and jumps off the hood as the other animal springs. Algenon fights back with its claws but is no match for the cat. After a few minutes, Algenon wrestles free and goes whimpering off down the road with the other beast in pursuit.

Soon all is silent. But you are *not* going to get out of the van.

Hurry to page 47.

38

You decide not to approach the costumed people. You go back along the trail. It's farther than you remembered. But finally you reach the campsite where your tent is pitched. Your parents' tent is still not there. You search around the clearing.

"Mom! Dad! Hel-lo!" you call out. "This isn't funny anymore!" But no one answers your cries.

You crawl back into your tent and try to go back to sleep, hoping that things will look brighter in the morning.

You doze off for a while. But then something wakes you up. It sounds like someone—or something—is creeping around your tent. It's definitely not the wind this time. You pull the covers over your head and try to block out the sound. But it won't go away.

Whatever it is is scratching along the base of your tent, trying to get in. You watch as it bumps against one of the tent poles, shaking the frame. You realize that you'd better get out before this thing, whatever it is, knocks the tent over.

Move it! Turn to page 25.

"Hurry up!" your mom yells. Her voice sounds high and squeaky.

You run over and take down your tent. You tie all the sections of rope together to make one long cord. Then you fasten one end to a tent peg driven deep into the ground far back from the pit, and toss the other end down into the hole.

"Your mother's coming up first!" your dad shouts. "I'll lift her partway."

You watch the rope go taut. The peg quivers.

You hold your breath.

What if the rope breaks? Your mom would never forgive you.

Hold your breath and turn to page 83.

40

"You made that up," you say impatiently. "I don't have time for kiddie jokes."

"Just come into our house and Mama and Papa will tell you."

"House? Do they work for the park?" you ask. If they live and work at the information center, they can help you find your parents.

The girl doesn't reply. She just stares at you.

You're not sure you should go inside. Maybe you should get away from this strange girl.

She's nothing to be afraid of.
Turn to page 23.

You decide to go somewhere else for help.
Turn to page 50.

The cell door opens and the sheriff shoves a tray through the door. On it are several bowls filled with a suspicious-looking mixture.

"Porridge!" Joshua says. "I'm finally getting something to eat. They grabbed me with the loaf of bread before I had nary a bite."

The other prisoners grab their bowls and start gulping down the food. Somehow, you've lost your appetite.

Sometime later, several men armed with muskets and led by the sheriff arrive at the door. They herd everyone out of the jail and down to the town square. In the center stands a large tree. Several ropes with nooses at the ends dangle from the branches. The other ends of the ropes are tied to horses standing nearby.

"The hangin' tree is ready," the sheriff announces, licking the corners of his mustache. "Let's get this over with."

Be brave and turn to page 57.

42

You move slowly in the direction of the lights. The clicking sound gets louder, and you hear a strange kind of music. It reminds you of something you've heard before, but you can't place it.

Now you can make out moving shapes. People are dancing around a large campfire, casting shadows on the trees. They look like they are rehearsing for a play or a circus. You creep up and peer cautiously through the bushes. In front of you is a circle of elaborately painted wagons around a wide clearing. Horses are tethered nearby.

Some of the men are playing violins while women click things in their hands in time to the music. That was the clicking noise you heard.

Maybe you should go over and talk to them. They look harmless enough. In fact, they seem to be having a good time.

If you go over to the strangely costumed people,
turn to page 26.

If you creep back into the forest,
turn to page 38.

You feel the blood pumping in your veins as you whiz past the trees and rocks. Thornbushes tear at your clothes and leave deep scratches on your arms and legs.

Gasping for breath, you stumble blindly through the forest. Behind you, you hear shouts and curses.

You splash madly through several small streams and follow what look like overgrown trails, but you have no idea where you are going. For all you know, you could be going around in circles.

Now the sun is low in the sky. It must be late afternoon. Everything is very quiet, except for the insects buzzing around your ears. You must be a long way from your campsite. If you can get to a *real* town, you can call your grandparents.

You spend another hour tramping through the woods looking for trails, the information center, or any state park structure. It starts to get dark. You're almost ready to collapse when you suddenly come out on a dirt road. It looks like the one that ran through the village.

Find out where you are on page 7.

44

Instead, the man looks at the dime suspiciously. Then he puts the edge between his teeth and bites down.

"What is this?" he asks angrily.

"Uh—it's a dime. Ten cents," you say, squirming in your chair. "You know. That's the price you have on the sign outside." Did you read the sign wrong?

"A ten-cent coin is made of silver," the man says angrily. "This isn't silver. And it has a strange face on it."

"That's President Roosevelt," you say. "That's what dimes have on them."

"What are you talking about? All proper coins have the face of King George on them. Passin' counterfeit coins is a capital offense in this colony. I'll have to hand you over to the sheriff for hangin'. There's a group hangin' this afternoon."

"Oh, I get it," you say with a laugh. "This is just a practical joke you play on tourists, right?"

"Tourists? 'Tis no joke," the man barks. "I'm the tavern keeper. And I won't stand for any nonsense."

Start to sweat on page 6.

46

"I think we've found our campsite," your mom says.

"Can I go exploring?" you ask. "Maybe some other people are camping nearby. I might find some kids."

"Not by yourself. You could get lost," your mom says. She's such a worrywart.

That evening you and your parents roast hot dogs stuck on long sticks over an open fire.

"When I was your age," your dad says, "I used to camp here with my dad and your uncle Joe."

"I know," you say, nodding. He's told you this story about ten times today.

"At night around the campfire, my dad used to tell Joe and me stories. Spooky stories."

"Tell one," you suggest. You know your dad is dying to.

"I don't know if I can remember them exactly," he says. You know he can. He's just drawing out the suspense. "They were mostly about kids lost in Wiley Woods. Kids who were never seen again." His eyes grow wide.

See them grow even wider on page 70.

Your mom and dad find you there in the morning.

"Whatever possessed you to sleep in the minivan?" your dad asks.

"I—I guess I was having a bad dream," you say. You must have been having a nightmare. The whole experience is too weird to have been true. "I—I felt safer in here."

Your dad smiles at you. "Well, you know you could always have joined me and Mom in our tent," he tells you.

"Uh, yeah. I guess so," you say.

"Of course you could have," your dad says. "Now let me tell you, the woods can be a strange place. It—"

But you aren't really paying attention to what your dad is saying. Instead, you're staring at a set of large animal tracks. Tracks that lead straight from the minivan to your tent. . . .

The End

48

A few seconds later, your parents dash out of their tent.

"What's the matter?" your dad shouts.

At the same time, Algenon bolts for the woods, carrying the collapsed tent, now clinging to its back, with it.

"What is that?" your mom cries. "Are you okay?"

"It looks like a small bear," your dad says, as Algenon, still carrying the tent, disappears into the woods. "How did it get into your tent?"

"It's a long story, Dad," you say.

The End

The girl looks a few years younger than you. Next to her is a furry four-legged animal on a leash. You can't tell if it's a large dog or a small bear. It looks like a combination of both.

"Algenon and I saw you wandering through the woods," she says.

"Well, I'm, uh, looking for my parents," you tell her. The girl is wearing a starched, flowered dress with patent leather shoes. She looks like she's going to a fancy party.

"My parents are inside arguing about whether we should rescue you," the girl says.

"Huh?" you say. This is very weird. "I don't need to be rescued, exactly. I just need to—"

"If you keep wandering through Wiley Woods, the goblins'll get you," she says solemnly.

"Yeah, right," you scoff.

"A goblin got my little sister after she wandered off. We found her bones gnawed clean and stacked in a pile," the girl tells you, her yellow eyes glowing.

Turn to page 40.

50

Your heart pounding, you dash back into the woods. That girl was just too weird. Your sneakers thud along the path as you try to put as much distance as possible between you and the information center.

Run. Run. Run. To your dismay, you realize you are off the trail. As you search around for it, pushing through the bushes, you find another path and follow it to a new clearing. You stop short. In the middle of the clearing is a crude statue, at least six feet tall.

It's a human figure holding something at arm's length. You move closer. It's a glass ball. You watch, mesmerized, as the ball rotates, reflecting the moonlight. It is strangely hypnotic.

You step a little closer. Slowly you stretch out your hand. Just one touch—

Suddenly the ground drops out from under you! You open your mouth to scream, but nothing comes out.

You slide down a deep, muddy incline and hit bottom with a splash.

Where are you?

Quick! Turn to page 14.

You sit on the ground for a while with your eyes tightly shut. "They're not real. They're not real," you chant to yourself, willing the ghost kids to disappear.

After a few minutes, you open one eye. Then the other. But the weird ghost kids are still there. Waiting for you.

"Are you ready to come with us?" asks the girl in the lacy dress. It's then that you notice that your arms and legs are glowing. You can see right through them.

You realize you have no choice.

You have become one of the ghost kids of Wiley Woods.

The End

52

"You look tired," the woman says. "Why don't you go upstairs and get a good night's sleep? We'll look for your parents in the morning."

"No! I want to find them now!" you holler. "You're the park rangers, aren't you? You're supposed to help people!"

The woman gives you a hurt look. "We *are* trying to help you," she snaps. "You did come to our house, you know."

"I must be having a nightmare," you say under your breath. "I wish I could wake up."

"Did you try the pinch test?" Amanda asks.

"Well, yes, I did," you say uneasily.

"Did you pinch your earlobe?" she presses.

"Earlobe? No, I—"

"Here, I'll pinch it for you," Amanda says. Before you can stop her, she reaches over and pinches you hard on the ear.

"Ow!" you cry out. "That hurt!"

They all look at you expectantly. "Did you wake up?" the woman asks.

Find out on page 66.

"I can explain this whole thing," you whimper. "The tavern keeper is making a big mistake. He—"

The sheriff doesn't give you a chance to finish. He shoves you into the building and slams the door behind you.

To your horror, you realize you are in a jail cell. It's small and dark, with a cracked stone floor and walls to match. There are several other people in the cell. Two are about your age.

"What'd they get you for?" a skinny, bug-eyed blond boy asks you.

"The tavern keeper claims I gave him a counterfeit coin, and—"

"Ooh, that be bad!" the boy says. "They'll hang you sure as anything for that."

"But it's *not* counterfeit," you say, taking out another dime from your pocket and handing it to the boy. He takes the coin and holds it up to the light at the window.

"This be a foreign coin—maybe Spanish?" he says, turning to you expectantly.

"No!" you cry. "It's American!"

Turn to page 29.

54

You've got to escape!

Fortunately, Amanda and her parents (or whoever they are) have gone to bed. You force your fingers and toes to move. Then you work on your arms and legs.

When your whole body is under your control again, you struggle to get loose from the quilt. It's wrapped around you like a straitjacket. You know it's silly, but it almost seems alive. Anything's possible in this place, you decide.

Don't give up. Turn to page 22.

"You'll believe in them if they catch you," Carlo says knowingly.

While you and Carlo have been talking, the music has stopped. The actors and dancers are loading things into their wagons and hitching up the horses.

"What's happening?" you ask.

"We must be out of the forest by dawn."

"Why? Where are you going?" you ask.

"We're following the trail to the town of Dunston. We must be there by morning to set up our stage. You are welcome to come along," Carlo offers.

You pace back and forth for a moment. "Will you pass by the information center where the park ranger lives?"

Carlo shrugs. "I don't know of any center. But you could ask the constable in Dunston about your parents."

"Constable? Is that like a policeman?" you ask.

Carlo looks puzzled. "Po-lice-man," he repeats, as if he's never heard the word before. "What's that?"

Is he kidding? Go to page 68.

A man shoves you next to one of the nooses and quickly slips it over your head. Another ties your hands loosely behind your back. You see the same procedure being repeated with the others.

A big crowd has gathered. People are wearing brightly colored clothes, as if dressed for a holiday. Some wave red and orange banners, while others carry large bouquets of flowers. You see Carlo in the crowd. He waves at you with a big smile.

Great, you think. My only friend around here and he's enjoying seeing me hang.

You hear a drumroll and see the sheriff swat the backs of the horses with a riding crop. Just as your horse is about to bolt away from the tree, you remember the pocketknife you brought with you on the camping trip—it's in your back pocket.

Is there still time to save your life?
Try it on page 65.

Is it all over? Don't hang around—turn to page 71.

58

"The goblins that live underground got him!" your dad shouts. He and your mom cling to each other as if they're watching a horror movie.

You roll your eyes. Your parents can be so childish sometimes. "Oh, that's really scary," you say, pretending to shiver.

Your dad ignores your sarcasm. "Anyway, campers reported seeing ghostly kids in the forest on moonlit nights. They were lonely, and sometimes they took other young campers against their will to keep them company."

"You and Uncle Joe made it out of Wiley Woods okay," you huff.

"*We* never left our parents," your dad says smugly.

Your mom helps you slide into your small tent. "Don't worry, we're close by," she says.

"I'm fine," you say. As if a story like that would scare you.

You lie in your sleeping bag, listening to the sound of the waterfall. Soon you hear your dad snoring. It's a comforting sound. You drift off to sleep.

Turn to page 9.

"I'd like to go with you, but I'd better go back to my campsite," you tell Carlo. "If my parents are back, they'll be worried about me."

"Good luck, then," Carlo says, waving goodbye as he runs to the back of a departing wagon.

You go back to the woods and begin to retrace your steps. Your feet are killing you. It seems like you've been walking for hours. Finally, you stop to rest in a clearing.

This is one strange night, you think, plopping down on a rotting tree stump. It's getting cold. You sure wish you had your sleeping bag. There are lots of dead leaves on the ground. Maybe you could make a little pile of them and lie down. They might keep you warm.

As you start to gather leaves, you notice that the ground around you is slowly growing lighter. At first you think it's moonlight. But the moon doesn't shine this brightly.

Turn to page 77.

60

You crawl out from under the bed next to the door and stand up. You glance back and see that the quilt is thrashing about. You hope it doesn't know where you are.

You slip on your shoes, open the door a crack, and look out. The hallway and the stairs are dark. There's just enough light to see by. You inch out through the door and creep down the stairs, staying close to the wall. You don't want the stairs to creak and wake anybody up.

When you reach the first floor, you race to the door and yank it open.

"Ahhh!" you scream. The park ranger is standing on the other side!

"You need to rest. Go back upstairs and lie down," he says in a mechanical voice.

But the electrical shocks you felt before have worn off. Your body is your own again.

Fight back on page 16.

"Ahhh!" you gasp, stumbling backward. You turn to run but trip on the underbrush. In a panic, you struggle to your feet. You look back and see that the dark creature is gone. You hear crashing sounds moving away from you at great speed. Whatever it is, it's as afraid as you are.

You take a deep breath. "Okay," you tell yourself. "Stay calm." Your parents must be *somewhere*. They wouldn't just leave you. For one thing, they love you. And for another, they're law-abiding citizens. They'd never abandon you!

You bend down to tie a loose shoelace and then keep going. Suddenly you hear voices again. Much closer. A man and a woman. It sounds like they are having a nasty argument.

Is it your parents?

You're not sure.

Nervously, you cross the clearing and continue along the narrow path through the woods. The voices are getting louder.

What's going on? Find out on page 13.

You look around in a panic. You're in another small clearing, surrounded by a circle of trees.

"Hey!" you scream as someone taps you on the back. You spin around but see nothing except the circle of trees.

Your eyes widen in horror when you realize that it wasn't a person that touched you. It was a tree! All the trees here have faces with human features. Mean ones.

"You shouldn't have come to our woods," hisses a tall, spindly oak.

"What are you going to do to me?" you ask, your knees shaking with fright.

"You'll find out soon enough." It's the goblin speaking. You gasp as the tiny man dashes toward you. He takes a long, glowing rope from his pocket and begins to wind it around you.

You can't move your arms or legs! The goblin has you encased in some kind of cocoon.

"Help! Let me go!" you scream. There's just a small opening left in front of your face.

Shake a leg, if you can, on page 72.

64

At the first light of dawn you open your eyes and see the man, the woman, and Amanda, all with cruel smiles on their faces, peering down at you. Your feet are tied together with rope, and your hands are bound tightly behind your back. You struggle to get loose.

"No way! Let me go!" you scream at the top of your lungs.

The woman shoves a large apple into your mouth. "It's so much fun running a state park this way, and it cuts down on the cost of food," she says brightly.

They lift you up and carry you downstairs.

"The last one we caught made a great stew," Amanda says, licking her lips.

"I don't feel like cutting this one up," the woman says. "We'll just bake it whole."

You manage to shake the apple out of your mouth. "Help! Help me!" you shriek.

Just then you hear something. It sounds like someone knocking at the front door. Maybe you'll be rescued!

If you think you're dreaming, turn to page 74.

If you still have hope, turn to page 27.

You cry out as you are yanked up off the ground. You shake your hands free of the rope. There! In a flash you reach up and slice your knife through the rope.

Boom! Your body slams down on the saddle of the horse as it gallops away at full speed from the astonished crowd.

Choking, you cling to the horse's neck as his hooves fly across the ground. Behind you, the angry cries of the crowd grow fainter and fainter.

You're lucky to be alive. But what will happen to you now?

The End

"No!" you cry.

"If it's only a dream, then nothing can really hurt you," says Amanda.

"Look," you plead. "I just want to find my parents. I woke up and went to their tent and they and it were gone. They must be in trouble!"

"You can't go anywhere tonight," the man says.

Now you are really getting mad. "I can do what I want!" you yell.

"Not in Wiley Woods," says the man. He points to the map again and laughs. "We're in charge here. You have to do whatever we tell you."

"Go upstairs!" the woman says, pointing to the stairway. "No more Mrs. Nice Gal from me!"

Amanda picks up a park map and sticks it in your hand. You feel a slight tremor run through your body. It's as if the paper is electrified!

Get shocked again on page 20.

You leave the wagon with Carlo and push through the good-natured crowd.

"We'll be here until sunset," Carlo calls over his shoulder before going his own way.

"I'll remember," you call back.

The people here must dress this way for the tourists, you say to yourself. But you don't see any tourists. Maybe the restored village isn't open for the day yet. A hand-painted sign hangs over a wide porch on one of the buildings. It says CROWN TAVERN. A smaller sign attached to the wall next to the front door says HEARTY BREAKFAST, TEN CENTS.

You've never heard of a breakfast being that cheap.

Luckily you have a bunch of change in your pocket. You go into the tavern and sit at a table next to the door.

"What'll you have?" asks a large, greasy-looking man wearing an oversized apron.

Give your order on page 73.

68

You stare at Carlo. "This isn't a time for jokes," you snap.

Carlo stares back at you. "I'm not making jokes," he says.

"Well, anyway, if we get to town I can use a telephone to call my grandparents and tell them what's happened," you say, more to yourself than Carlo.

Carlo gives you another blank look.

"You *do* know what a telephone is, don't you?" you say impatiently.

"A tel-e-phone?" Carlo breaks out in a big smile. "Oh, yes. It's a big horn you shout through. But the sound won't carry more than a tenth of a league."

A league? What's that? You decide not to ask. You look around and see that some of the wagons are already moving out.

Do you feel like sticking with Carlo?
If so, turn to page 36.

Or would you rather go solo?
Then turn to page 59.

You look wildly around for the park sign and entrance. But all you see is the dirt road you're traveling on. A freshly posted notice is stuck to a nearby tree. You run over to see what it says.

THE ANNUAL TOWN MEETING
WILL BE HELD ON JULY 1, 1680

"Sixteen—sixteen-eighty," you squeak. You really are in a time warp!

"Hurry up, we're leaving!" Carlo motions to you from the wagon. The wagons start up again, taking you to a new and surprising life as a traveling juggler.

The End

"Why? What happened to them?" you ask.

"Well, the park used to have very strict rules. No one under the age of fourteen was allowed to go out unsupervised. It was for safety reasons—there are a lot of steep cliffs and heavily wooded areas around here. It's dangerous." Your dad looks at you meaningfully. "But some kids wouldn't listen," he continues. "And they went out alone."

"Wasn't there some strange story about fog?" asks your mom. "I remember hearing about it."

"Yeah," says your dad. "Supposedly there were these weird mist circles. No one could figure out what they were. But if you accidentally stepped in one, it could suck you down into who knows what." He shivers. "I never saw one, but Uncle Joe did. He still claims that he saw a boy sucked in right before his eyes." He shakes his head. "Poor kid."

Your mom wraps her arms around herself. "And you know what probably happened then?" she whispers.

Find out on page 58.

Your bound hands fumble for the knife. Then you feel its smooth surface. You pull it out of your pocket and . . . Oh, no! You've dropped it!

The horse bolts forward. You scream as the rope tightens around your neck.

Tighter. Tighter. You can't breathe. It's choking you! You struggle valiantly for air. The voices of the crowd ring in your ear.

Turn to page 80.

"Too late for that!" the goblin says as he pushes you toward a glowing circle of light on the forest floor. "I've just the place for you."

"No!" you cry. "My parents will be looking for me. They'll—"

The goblin grabs your shoulder. "Shut up and hold still while I finish," he cackles, covering your mouth with a gooey liquid. He shoves you into the circle of light.

"Good-bye, good-bye!" shriek the trees. Your knees quiver as the ground begins to shake. You feel yourself start to spin, slowly at first, then faster and faster in a circle. The light is pulling you down—it's as if you are being sucked into the ground.

"Hee hee hee!" giggles the goblin.

It's the last thing you hear!

The End

"I'll take the ten-cent breakfast," you say with a smile.

"Comin' up with all the trimmin's," he says, retreating to the kitchen in the back.

You look around the tavern while you wait. It's not very busy. Everyone is wearing old-fashioned clothes. You glance down at your shirt and jeans self-consciously.

A few minutes later, the man reappears carrying a tray covered with dishes of eggs, ham slices, potatoes, corn, and a large mug of tea.

"Thanks a lot," you say. This is the best thing that's happened to you all weekend. It's more food than you can eat, but you do your best.

When you've finished, you signal the man over to your table and hand him a dime. And you leave two pennies on the table for a tip. Your dad always leaves twenty percent for the server. You smile broadly.

But the man doesn't smile back.

Find out why on page 44.

74

You're right. You *were* dreaming. No one has come to rescue you.

Amanda opens the door of a very large oven. The last thing you feel is a sudden blast of heat as the weird family tosses you inside. And for you, it's . . .

The End

You laugh, too. "*I'm* strange?"

The inside of the wagon is quite roomy. The front part is taken up by a large double bed raised several feet off the floor. Under it are shelves and drawers for storage. A curved ceiling made of wooden strips and lined with heavy cloth arches over the top.

Carlo scrambles up onto the bed. "Come up here and get some rest," he says.

You climb up a small ladder and lie down on the other side of him. The wagon bounces under you, but the bed is soft and you are pretty tired. You quickly doze off.

Turn to page 84.

You look up. Through the tree branches, you see lots of small glowing circles. They look almost like beach balls.

What are they?

Slowly they descend to the ground. As the first one touches the earth, the ball pops and a girl in a long lacy dress stands in front of you. She glows with a soft, bluish light. To your amazement, you can see right through her to the trees at the edge of the clearing!

"Do you want to become one of us?" she asks in a musical voice.

"One of you?" you whisper. "Who are you?"

The girl laughs. "Look around."

The other brightly glowing balls are floating down. As each one reaches the ground, it turns into a transparent kid.

"We were all lost in the forest," the girl says. "Now we're ghosts. Do you want to hang out with us?"

Give your answer on page 17.

"What did you do to my parents!" you scream, letting the rope slacken. The goblin kicks and flails his legs in the air.

"You'd better let me up—or you'll never know," snarls the goblin.

You bite your lip. Can you trust him?

Suddenly you hear someone call your name.

You look behind you. Your parents are running your way.

"Mom! Dad!" you cry, forgetting all about the goblin as you let go of the rope and hug your parents. "You'll never believe what happened!" You tell them the whole story. Your dad shines a flashlight down into the hole. The goblin has disappeared.

The story seems too crazy to be true. But your parents believe you. Because there, stuck on the tree root, is a yellow cap.

Maybe you should take it for a souvenir. Because this story has reached . . .

The End

"How did you manage to get the sheet wrapped around your neck like that?" asks your mom.

"Wha—" you mumble, turning your head.

"You must have been tossing and turning all night!"

You open your eyes and look up. No rope. No horse. Only your mom and dad, crouching down and peering into your tent. You've never been so glad to see them in your life!

The End

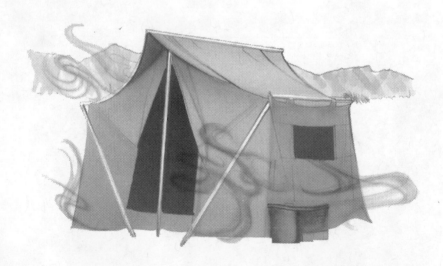

A few people hear him and start to chase you as well. One of them, a portly man with a red face, tries to block your way. You dart around him. He makes a grab for you.

"No way!" you scream, giving him a shove. He trips over his own feet and falls to the ground. You take off, running as fast as you can down the road.

In a few minutes you reach the edge of town. The road curves to the right and goes off through the woods. For a brief moment you are out of sight of the pursuing villagers. You plunge into the woods.

Don't stop! Turn to page 43.

82

You yank back your hand. "Brrr! You're freezing!" you say.

"I know," the girl says. "But if you're a ghost like me, you don't feel the cold."

"I'm not like you," you say, moving back. "And I'm not lost!"

"Oh, but you are. We know."

You shrink back in fear as the ghost kids form a circle around you.

"We won't hurt you," one boy tells you, reaching out to touch your shoulder.

You try to duck and fall backward. "Leave me alone!" you shout. You remember your dad's story about the lost children turning into ghosts. Maybe you're just having a nightmare. That's why your parents' tent disappeared—none of this is real!

Or is it? Turn to page 51.

Luckily it holds.

Or is it "luckily"? Your mom's head and arms appear at the top of the hole. You blink. Since when did your mom wear a yellow cap and red silk shirt to bed? She normally wears plaid flannel pajamas.

But this *isn't* your mom. It's a goblin! He disguised his voice to make you *think* he was your mom.

Quick! Turn back to page 78.

84

Sunlight streaming through the windows at the back of the wagon wakes you up the next morning. The wagon is still bouncing along.

"Carlo?" you call out. You climb down the ladder and look out through one of the windows, hoping to see the information center. Instead, you find that you are just entering a small town. On both sides are one-story buildings with thatched roofs. There are no cars or buses—just some horses tied up in front of the houses and open wagons.

Rub your eyes and turn to page 8.